Collins

Mugge

---

by

Andrew Payne

Resource Material by
Suzy Graham-Adriani
and
Anthony Banks

William Collins' dream of knowledge for all began with the publication of his first book in 1819. A self-educated mill worker, he not only enriched millions of lives, but also founded a flourishing publishing house. Today, staying true to this spirit, Collins books are packed with inspiration, innovation and a practical expertise. They place you at the centre of a world of possibility and give you exactly what you need to explore it.

Collins. Do more.

Published by Collins
An imprint of HarperCollins*Publishers*
77–85 Fulham Palace Road
Hammersmith
London
W6 8JB

Commissioned by Charlie Evans
Design by JPD
Cover design Charlotte Wilkinson
Cover illustration by Steve Web
Production by Katie Butler
Printed and bound by Martins the Printers

Browse the complete Collins catalogue
at www.collinseducation.com

Acknowledgements
Text credits: p78–79, extracts taken from sportsrelief.com; p80–81, extract from *Face* by Benjamin Zephaniah (2002) is reproduced with permission of Bloomsbury Publishing PLC; p82 and 87–88, extracts from *Noughts and Crosses* by Malorie Blackman (2002) are reproduced with permission of Corgi Childrens' Books, a division of Random House Publishers; Extract from *Fear and Fashion* is taken from www.crimereduction.gov.uk, Lemos and Crane 2002.

Photo credits: p66 Anthony Banks

Contents

PLAYSCRIPT

RESOURCES

Characters

DIG	a 15-year-old schoolboy
MARKY	a 15-year-old schoolboy
TAYLOR	a 15-year-old schoolboy
MEL	a 15-year-old schoolgirl
SOPH	a 15-year-old schoolgirl
LEON	a 15-year-old schoolboy
TV REPORTER	middle-aged, male or female
NEWSREADER 1	middle-aged, male or female
NEWSREADER 2	middle-aged, male or female
GAWPER 1	bystander, any age
GAWPER 2	bystander, any age
GAWPER 3	bystander, any age
POLICE OFFICER	middle-aged, male or female
VICAR	middle-aged, male or female
ENSEMBLE	providing crowd scenes, congregation, atmosphere

Mugged

Scene One

*Two park benches facing the audience, as far apart as the stage allows.
Between the benches lies a beaten-up litter bin with more rubbish lying
around it than in it, and a sign: 'ALBION PARK. PART OF THE ALBION
COUNCIL GREEN SPACE INITIATIVE. NO BALL GAMES, NO CYCLING.'
Little of this may be legible as the sign is covered with graffiti. Off, a police
siren wails.*

*Enter **Dig**, a scruffy kid carrying a bag or backpack. Eating from a giant bag
of crisps almost as big as he is. Jumps on the left-hand bench. (Left and right
are from the audience's point of view throughout.) **Dig** stands on tiptoe,
peers over the heads of the audience for a moment or two, then jumps down,
sits. Eats crisps.*

*Enter **Marky**, spectacularly scruffy, also carrying a bag. Drinking a giant
milkshake. (All the characters attend the same school. Whatever else they're
wearing, they all wear white shirts and school ties, the ties knotted in
various bizarre ways.)*

DIG   Alright?

MARKY   Alright?

***Marky** jumps on the left-hand bench, goes through the same routine as **Dig**,
peering over the audience.*

DIG   Are they there?

MARKY   No.

***Marky** jumps down, sits next to **Dig**. A beat while **Marky** drinks milkshake
through the straw and **Dig** eats crisps.*

MARKY	Breakfast, the most important meal of the day.

*They swap. **Marky** eats crisps, **Dig** sucks on the straw – and gets a surprise.*

DIG	*(appalled)* Oh man!
MARKY	Good or what?
DIG	That is disgusting! What is it?
MARKY	You get a chocolate milkshake, drink half of it, top it up with Coke.
DIG	Oh man! It went up my nose!
MARKY	I haven't decided what to call it yet.
DIG	How about 'Puke'? How about 'Puke Up Your Nose'?
MARKY	You love it really.

***Dig** has another drink.*

DIG	Actually, that is wicked.
MARKY	Told you.

They swap back. Eat, drink.

DIG	This is bad, what we're eating. We're going to be a health statistic.
MARKY	No, this is good. Protein, carbohydrates, vitamin C.
DIG	Chemicals. Preservatives.
MARKY	I've got a theory about preservatives.
DIG	What?
MARKY	They put preservatives in food to make it last longer, right.
DIG	So?

MARKY	So why shouldn't they make *us* last longer?
DIG	Brilliant.
MARKY	All the crap we eat, we'll probably live forever.
DIG	Brilliant, Marky.
MARKY	I rest my case.

Dig checks his watch.

DIG	It's ten past. We ought to go if we're going round.
MARKY	Are they there?

Dig gets up on the bench, peers into the distance.

DIG	No.
MARKY	We'll go across then. Plenty of time.

Dig sits back down.

DIG	We ought to go round the park, Marky, just in case. If you're late again, you're going to get suspended.
MARKY	There's plenty of time if we go across.

Beat.

DIG	The last time I got mugged, my mum didn't believe me. She thought I made it up to get more money off her. And I've only got two quid today.
MARKY	All right, all right, we'll go *round*, okay?
DIG	We ought to go then, it takes longer.
MARKY	Dig, man, relax, there's loads of time.

Beat.

You get anything?

DIG	Yeah.

Dig rummages in his backpack. Takes out a small box, hands it to Marky.

DIG	From the art shop.
MARKY	Cool. What is it?
DIG	It's like a special art knife. For cutting stuff. You know, art stuff.
MARKY	Cool.

Marky hands back the box.

DIG	I thought there were felt-tips in it, but I didn't have time to look. The bloke in there, he's really suspicious. What about you?

Marky rummages in his backpack, produces a pack of fags.

MARKY	Twenty Marlboro.
DIG	Swap you.
MARKY	You don't smoke, Dig.
DIG	Neither do you!
MARKY	That's not the point!
DIG	Twenty Marlboro for a special art knife. It's a brilliant deal!
MARKY	Dig, man, I don't do art! And you don't smoke!
DIG	Well, maybe I'm going to start.
MARKY	Why would you want to do that?
DIG	Because I'm stressed!
MARKY	*(bewildered)* What are you stressed about?
DIG	Everything. School, home – and them!

Dig points into the distance, over the audience.

MARKY	The muggers aren't there today.
DIG	So they'll be there tomorrow. Or the day after! Come on, Marky, a special art knife for twenty fags. What's your problem?
MARKY	What do you want them for?
DIG	I told you, I'll probably smoke them.
MARKY	No you won't, you want to give them to Soph.
DIG	*(embarrassed)* Shut up, Marky.
MARKY	Admit you want to give them to Soph, then I'll swap.
DIG	All right. Give us them, then.
MARKY	You got to say it, man!
DIG	I want to give them to Soph, all right?
MARKY	Well, I don't want to stand in the way of your future happiness.

They swap.

MARKY	Though frankly, Dig, speaking as your friend, I don't think twenty Marlboro is going to do it. Of all the doomed relationships in the world, you and Soph are *so* doomed.
DIG	I know.

Off, the sound of girls singing, laughing. And a boy's voice, loud and assertive.

DIG	It's Taylor.

They hurriedly hide the knife and fags in their bags.

*Taylor enters, followed by **Mel** and **Soph**. **Mel** and **Soph** arm in arm, singing something current. Doesn't matter if they're any good. Both carrying phones, **Soph** is texting as she sings. **Taylor** could be older than **Dig** and **Marky**, or could be the same age. Either way, he's bigger, better dressed, full of himself. **Soph** and **Mel** also seem older than **Marky** and **Dig**.*

*Taylor jumps on the right-hand bench, has a quick look into the distance, then jumps down, goes over to **Dig** and **Marky** on the left-hand bench.*

TAYLOR	Oi, off my bench, dossers.
DIG	I thought *that* was your bench.
TAYLOR	It was yesterday. Today, this is my bench.

*Dig reluctantly gets to his feet, clutching his crisps and his bag. **Marky** doesn't move.*

MARKY	Actually, Tayl, these benches are the property of the local council, therefore legally belonging to all of us…

*Taylor grabs **Marky** and drags him roughly off the bench.*

TAYLOR	Off, you little dosser. I'm not in the mood for you this morning.
MARKY	All right, all right. Watch the jacket, would you, it's Goochi.

*Taylor slumps on the left-hand bench. **Marky** and **Dig** shuffle over to the right-hand bench, passing **Mel** and **Soph** who are making their way to join **Taylor**.*

MARKY	Alright, Mel?
MEL	Alright, Marky?
DIG	Alright, Soph?
SOPH	*(as she texts)* Looking good, Dig.
DIG	Thanks.

SOPH	I'm lying.
DIG	I know.
MARKY	Devastating repartee, Dig.
DIG	I know.

Mel sits down next to Taylor who flings a proprietorial arm round her. Marky and Dig sit on the right-hand bench. Soph, still texting, sits on the left-hand bench. Mel shoves Taylor off, climbs onto the bench, peers into the distance.

DIG	*(to Mel)* Anyone there?
MEL	No.

Mel gets down, sits. Checks her watch.

MEL	*(to Soph)* We ought to go.
SOPH	*(still texting)* There's loads of time.
MARKY	*(to Mel)* Hey, Mel. We're going across the park. Want to come with us?
DIG	*(worried)* No we're not, we're going round!
MARKY	*(ignoring him)* Hey Soph, we're going across this morning. If you want to come, me and Dig will look after you.

Soph, Mel and Taylor laugh.

TAYLOR	That's funny, man.
DIG	*(worried)* We're not going across, we're going round!
SOPH	*(to Mel, holding up her phone)* The bastard won't answer me.
MEL	Bastard.
DIG	*(to Taylor)* Hey, Tayl. You going across?

*Taylor gets up, struts over to **Marky** and **Dig** on the right-hand bench.*

TAYLOR	Why, want me to protect you from the *gangsters*?
DIG	No.
TAYLOR	Want me to hold your girlie hands?
MARKY	No thanks, Tayl, you're not my type.
DIG	*(to **Taylor**)* Serious, Tayl, are you going across? 'Cos we're going to be late.
TAYLOR	I'm not going anywhere man, I've got a free lesson.
MARKY	No you haven't. You've got Mr Gillespie.
TAYLOR	Same thing.
MARKY	How come Mr Gillespie never suspends *you*?
TAYLOR	'Cos I turn up *enough*. You *never* turn up. That's the difference. It's politics, man. See what I'm saying? That's why I'm going to be rich and you're going to be a dosser.

Taylor does a pathetic wino shuffle across the stage.

TAYLOR	Big Ishoo! Big Ishoo!
MARKY	*(to **Dig**)* He's hilarious, isn't he?

*The refrain is taken up by **Soph** and **Mel**.*

TAYLOR	Big Ishoo! Help the poor dosser! Big Ishoo!

*During this, **Dig** stands on the right-hand bench, peers into the distance.*

DIG	They're there!

This shuts everyone up and has them standing on the benches immediately.

MEL	Where?

DIG	There. By the playground.
SOPH	That's not them.
TAYLOR	That's some old geezer.
DIG	No, not him. Over *there*.
MEL	Where?
MARKY	There's no one there, Dig.

*They all get down except **Dig** who's still looking.*

DIG	I'm sure I saw them.

*Enter **Leon**. Big as **Taylor**. A bully. Struts to left-hand bench and **Taylor**, **Mel** and **Soph**.*

TAYLOR	Alright, Leon?
LEON	Alright, Tayl?
SOPH	Hey Leon…

***Soph** gets up and confronts **Leon**.*

SOPH	I was texting you all last night!
LEON	So?
SOPH	Where were you?
LEON	I was busy.
SOPH	Busy? Busy doing what?
LEON	Stuff.
SOPH	What stuff?
LEON	Just stuff, alright girl?
MARKY	*(to **Dig**)* Hasn't he got a way with words.
DIG	Yeah, it's poetry.

MARKY	You can't compete with poetry, Dig.
DIG	No way.

*Leon walks over to the right-hand bench, looms threateningly over **Marky** and **Dig**.*

LEON	What?
DIG/MARKY	Nothing, Leon.
LEON	Give us a crisp, then.

*Leon grabs **Dig**'s big bag of crisps, now about half full, and takes a big handful. **Dig** gets off the bench, tries to get them back.*

DIG	Give 'em back, Leon.

*Leon backs away, ducking and dodging, as **Dig** makes half-hearted attempts to grab the crisps. **Leon** stuffing his mouth to overflowing as he taunts **Dig**.*

LEON	Umm delicious!
DIG	You're wasting them…
LEON	*(spraying crisps)* Umm my favourite!

*Dig makes a last attempt to grab the bag. **Leon** crumples it in his hands, crushing the remaining crisps, chucks the bag away. **Taylor**, **Mel** and **Soph** laugh. **Dig** retrieves the bag, peers inside, crestfallen.*

DIG	Thanks, Leon…
SOPH	Hey, got any fags, Tayl?
TAYLOR	No.

*Leon grabs **Dig**.*

LEON	*(searching him)* Got any fags?
DIG	No.

LEON	You sure?
MARKY	He doesn't smoke, Leon.
LEON	*(to Marky)* Keep your dosser nose out of it.
MARKY	You shouldn't either, it'll restrict your growth, it'll restrict the growth of your brain, which in your case will be a disaster 'cos you already need a high power microscope to find it…

Leon drops Dig and grabs Marky, throws him on the ground.

LEON	You'd better show some respect, you pikey little minger…

Leon jumps on top of Marky, hits him. Marky yells in pain. Dig hovers nervously.

DIG	Leave him alone, Leon.
MEL/SOPH	Yeah, leave him alone.

Leon goes through Marky's pockets.

LEON	Fifty pee? That all you got, you loser?

Leon gives Marky one last thump and gets off him. Marky lies on the ground. Leon turns on Dig.

LEON	Got any money?
DIG	No.
LEON	Liar.

He grabs Dig.

MEL	Leave him alone, Leon. Tell him to leave him alone, Soph.
SOPH	It's nothing to do with me…

*Soph gets up, goes over to shout in **Leon**'s face.*

SOPH	I DON'T CARE WHAT HE DOES ANYMORE!

*Leon ignores her. **Soph** flounces over to the right-hand bench and sits. **Leon** shakes **Dig**.*

LEON	How much?
DIG	Two quid.
LEON	Gimme.

*Dig reluctantly gropes in his pocket, **Leon** holding on to him, and takes out some coins. Hands them to **Leon**. **Marky**, on the ground, sits up.*

MARKY	You should do something about this violent behaviour, Leon. You should discuss it with your therapist.
LEON	*(puzzled)* Therapist? I haven't got a therapist.
MARKY	I rest my case.

Leon raises his fist.

LEON	Want some more?
MARKY	No, thank you, Leon, thanks very much for the kind offer – aaah!

*As **Leon** hits him anyway, then turns to **Soph** who's still sitting on the right-hand bench.*

LEON	Come here.
SOPH	I'm not talking to you! Hey Mel, let's go, we're going to be late.
LEON	Come here, slag!
SOPH/MEL	*(furious)* Don't call me that!/Don't call her that!

LEON	I'm sorry my love, my dearest darling, please come and sit down with me on the other bench…

Leon extends his hand. *Soph* reluctantly takes it, stands.

LEON	… slag!

Taylor laughs. *Soph* tries to hit *Leon*.

SOPH	Loser!

But *Soph* still allows herself to be led to the left-hand bench where *Mel* tussles angrily with *Taylor*. *Soph* and *Leon* sit next to them, *Soph* pushing and pulling angrily at *Leon*. The tussling between the two couples becomes more flirtatious. *Marky* and *Dig* watch this from the right-hand bench, sharing the last of *Marky*'s milkshake.

DIG	I don't get it. Why do they like those morons?
MARKY	I've got a theory about that.
DIG	What?
MARKY	It's their dads.
DIG	What do you mean?
MARKY	Girls, right, if their dad treats them like dirt, they think that's normal. So if you're nice to them, they think you're weird.
DIG	You mean Mel likes Tayl because he's like her dad?
MARKY	That's my theory.
DIG	And Soph likes Leon because *he's* like *her* dad? You're joking!
MARKY	Not *exactly* like him. Just bits. Certain aspects of behaviour. Mind you, I've never met Soph's dad. Or Mel's, for that matter. Thank God!
DIG	What about us?

MARKY	Same thing. Down to our mums.
DIG	That is such total crap! I like Soph and she isn't like my mum!
MARKY	On the contrary, there are many similarities.

*A spat flares up on the left-hand bench between **Soph** and **Leon**. **Soph** gets to her feet, hurling abuse at **Leon**.*

DIG	My mum ignores me. When she's not ignoring me, she shouts at me.

***Soph** looks over, sees **Marky** and **Dig** watching her.*

SOPH	*(to **Marky** and **Dig**, shouting)* What are you looking at, dossers?
MARKY	I so rest my case.
DIG	You're wrong, man. Watch.

***Dig** gets the cigarettes out of his backpack, goes over to the left-hand bench.*

DIG	Hey, Soph. Do you want some fags?
SOPH	*(suspicious)* You what?

***Dig** offers her the Marlboros.*

DIG	Do you want these? I don't need them.
SOPH	You sure?
DIG	Go on.
SOPH	*(shrugs)* All right.

***Soph** takes the cigarettes.*

TAYLOR	You got to give him something in return, Soph.
SOPH	Get lost, Tayl.

| TAYLOR | Twenty Marlboro, got to be worth a feel. |

*Leon laughs, high-fives **Taylor**.*

| SOPH | Pig! *(to **Dig**)* Thanks, Dig… |

*Impulsively, **Soph** kisses **Dig**, much to **Dig**'s surprise. Laughs and jeers from **Mel** and **Taylor**. **Leon** is annoyed.*

| TAYLOR | Aah. How sweet is that? |
| MEL | Yeuch, she kissed a dosser! |

*Leon aims a kick at **Dig** as he walks back to the right-hand bench.*

| LEON | Get out of here! |

*Dig sits down next to **Marky**.*

| DIG | *(to **Marky**)* See? I was nice to her and she didn't think it was weird. |
| MARKY | Trust me, she did. |

Leon gets up, goes over to the right-hand bench.

LEON	You told me you didn't have any fags.
DIG	I forgot.
LEON	Where d'you get them from?
DIG	Bought them.
LEON	Lying little dosser. You've been thieving again, haven't you?
DIG	No!
LEON	What else you got?
DIG	Nothing.

Soph	Leave him alone, Leon.
Leon	*(to **Marky**)* What about you, Big Ishoo. You been nicking stuff too? Got any goodies in there? *(pointing at his bag)*
Marky	No, nothing.
Leon	Let's have a look then.

*Leon grabs **Marky**'s bag. They wrestle with it for a beat or two.*

Soph	*(looking at her watch)* Omigod, omigod!
Leon	What?

*Distracted, **Leon** lets go of **Marky**'s bag.*

Soph	The time! I've got to go! I'm supposed to get in early to help Miss Ransom. She'll kill me! Mel, you coming?
Mel	Yeah, I'm coming.
Marky	You going across, Soph?
Soph	Course we are.
Marky	We'll come with you.
Dig	We're going round, Marky!
Marky	It's too late now, we'll have to go across. It's all right, we'll go with Soph and Mel.
Dig	*They'll* be all right, 'cos the muggers don't pick on *them*, they only pick on us!
Taylor	Yeah, 'cos you're *kids*, man. Little kids.

***Marky** has climbed onto the right-hand bench.*

Leon	Time you grew up, losers.
Marky	Anyway, they're not there today.

*Dig joins **Marky** up on the bench, peers. **Mel** and **Soph** are gearing themselves up to leave.*

MARKY   Hey, Soph! Can we go with you?

SOPH   Yeah, I suppose.

Marky jumps down, grabs his bag.

MARKY   Come on, Dig!

Dig stays on the bench, peers a bit longer.

DIG   I dunno… Leon, are you going across?

*Leon and **Taylor** are lounging on left-hand bench.*

LEON   Me? I'm not going anywhere.

TAYLOR   We got Gillespie, haven't we?

MARKY   Let's go, Dig.

*Dig gets down from the bench, picks up his bag. Dragging his heels. **Mel** and **Soph** are about to leave. **Mel** realises they are setting off with **Marky** and **Dig** in tow.*

MEL   Hey, I'm not walking across the park with you two!

SOPH   It's all right, Mel.

MEL   No way! Walk across the park with those losers! You're joking me!

SOPH   *(to **Marky** and **Dig**)* You'd better go round the park, then you'll be all right.

*Mel and **Soph** exit.*

LEON   Yeah, go round the kids' way.

MARKY   If I go round, I'll be late, I'll be suspended…

TAYLOR/LEON	Big Ishoo! Big Ishoo!
MARKY	Sod it, I'm going across.
DIG	We can still go round and get there in time if we run!
MARKY	Run? No way.
DIG	Marky…
MARKY	It's all right, the muggers aren't there. You coming, Dig?

Dig in an agony of indecision.

DIG	No.

Taylor and Leon make chicken noises.

MARKY	Okay. Laters.

Marky exits. Dig gets on the right-hand bench, stands on tip-toe, peers. Taylor and Leon gambol around Dig, making chicken noises. Dig ignores them until:

DIG	They're there! The muggers are there!

Taylor jumps onto the bench. Leon slumps on the other bench, unimpressed.

LEON	They're always there.
TAYLOR	Where?
DIG	*(pointing)* There! Coming out of the playground!
LEON	The girls'll be all right. They won't stop the girls.
DIG	*(shouting)* Marky!
TAYLOR	He hasn't seen them.
DIG	There's three of them!

Leon	Three?

Leon jumps onto the bench.

Taylor	Who is that?
Dig	It's the old geezer I saw. He's with the muggers. *(shouting)* Marky!
Taylor	He is big, man!
Leon	He ain't that big.
Dig	*(shouting)* Marky, come back!
Taylor	Who is he?
Dig	Marky's seen them. He's coming back! Run, Marky!
Taylor	The girls haven't seen them. *(shouting)* Oi, Mel! Soph! Come back!
Dig	They're stopping the girls!

Marky enters on the run, gasping for breath. Hurls his bag to the ground, climbs on the bench.

Marky	There's three of them!
Dig	The big bloke's got Soph.
Marky	They've got her phone!
Taylor	Oh man!

Leon jumps off the bench, runs downstage.

Leon	*(shouting)* You touch her, you're dead, man!
Taylor	Run, Mel!
Leon	*(shouting)* I'll kill you, you thieving bastard!
Dig	The girls are coming back!

Mel enters on the run.

MEL   They got her phone!

*Followed by **Soph**. **Soph** is in tears.*

SOPH   They got my phone!

***Leon** tries to put his arms round **Soph**. **Taylor** jumps down off the bench.*

LEON   You alright, babe?

SOPH   *(shoving him off)* Of course I'm not all right, they got my phone!

MEL   Who was that other one? I never seen him before. He was like twenty!

TAYLOR   *(to **Mel**)* You okay?

MEL   Yeah, no thanks to you!

TAYLOR   What was I supposed to do?

MEL   You could've done something!

TAYLOR   How? We were over here!

***Dig** and **Marky** are still on the bench, peering.*

DIG   They're walking back to the playground.

MARKY   They might at least have the decency to run.

LEON   *(shouting)* You're dead, man!

MARKY   *(wind up)* He heard you, Leon! He's coming over!

LEON   *(alarmed, takes a step back)* What?

MARKY   *(nudging **Dig**)* No, he's not, my mistake.

SOPH   *(distraught)* It was my mum's phone!

LEON   What?

24

MEL	It was her *mum's* phone!
SOPH	I took it this morning, there was no money on mine 'cos I was texting you all night!

Soph hurls herself at **Leon**, *punching him on the chest.*

LEON	It's not my fault!
SOPH	*(crying)* My mum'll kill me! She'll chuck me out! She said the next time I do anything, I have to go and live with my dad!
MEL	*(to Taylor)* Tayl, you've got to do something.
TAYLOR	What? What can I do?
MEL	Get her phone back!
SOPH	*(to Leon)* You've got to get my mum's phone back!
LEON	Where are they?

Marky and **Dig** *are still on the bench, peering.*

DIG	They're in the playground.
MARKY	Sitting on the swings.
TAYLOR	That geezer, he's a big bastard.
SOPH	The other two are only *kids*!
MEL	*(to Taylor)* Go with Leon, it's two against one!
TAYLOR	He must be like *twenty-five* or something!
LEON	*(to Soph)* What's the point? Me and Tayl go over, they'll just run away.
MARKY	You wish.
LEON	What?
TAYLOR	Who is that big geezer, anyway? I've never seen him before.

MEL	Me neither.
SOPH	I don't think he's from round here.
TAYLOR	I've never seen him before. *(to Leon)* You seen him before, Leon?
LEON	No, I haven't seen him before.
MARKY	I have.

This gets everyone's attention. **Marky** *jumps down from the bench.*

LEON	Who is he then?
MARKY	I think his name's Carl. Or Kyle. Something like that. His mum lives next door to mine. I've seen him round the flats.
TAYLOR	You *know* him?
MARKY	No, I don't know him, Tayl, we're not mates. I've just seen him round the flats.
LEON	You ever talk to him?
MARKY	No, but my mum talks to his mum.
DIG	We could tell the police… *(huge derision at this)*
LEON	They're not going to get Soph's phone back, are they?
TAYLOR	He'll know we grassed him up, he'll come straight back here looking for us.
LEON	And what if he recognised Marky? *(to Marky)* Did he recognise you, Marky?
MARKY	Dunno.

They start talking over each other.

MEL	He knows where Marky lives…
SOPH	*(crying)* My mum's going to throw me out…

26

TAYLOR	Over a poxy phone? You're joking me…
MEL	She will, too…
SOPH	You don't know what she's like…
LEON	She's a nutter, man…
TAYLOR	Get over it girl, you ain't going to get it back now…
MEL	*(shoves **Taylor**)* You get over it…
TAYLOR	Hey…
SOPH	*(to **Leon**, crying, hitting him)* She is not a nutter…
MARKY	I'll talk to him, Soph, all right?

This shuts them up.

DIG	What?
MARKY	I'll go and talk to him.
SOPH	You will?
MARKY	Yeah. I'll explain.
LEON	Explain what?
MARKY	About her mum's phone, what do you think?
LEON	Yeah, but what good will that do?
TAYLOR	Yeah, what good will that do?
MARKY	His mum knows my mum, all right? Maybe he'll give it back. As a favour.
MEL	Yeah, he might, mightn't he?
SOPH	Yeah, if you're like a mate of his?
DIG	He just said, he's not a *mate*.
MEL	Yeah, but you know him.
MARKY	Sort of.

SOPH	Thanks, Marky.
DIG	What if they mug you, man?
MARKY	I haven't got anything, have I? No money, no phone, nothing.
SOPH	Maybe Leon and Tayl should go with you.
MARKY	No, they'll think we're looking for a ruck.
TAYLOR	Yeah, they'd do a runner, man.
LEON	Soon as they saw us.
MARKY	*(to **Dig**)* Where are they?
DIG	Still in the playground.

Marky picks up his bag.

MARKY	*(to **Soph**)* I'll see you back at school, all right?

Dig gets down off the bench.

DIG	Marky, you want me to come with you?
MARKY	No, stay here, Dig.
DIG	Marky man, you sure?
MARKY	It's all right, I know the geezer. Anyway, I've got a theory.
DIG	What?
MARKY	Tell you later.

Marky exits. The others all climb on the benches to watch.

TAYLOR	Where are they? I can't see them.
DIG	In the playground. They've gone round by the climbing frame.
MEL	Someone should've gone with him.

TAYLOR		We offered.
SOPH		No you didn't, Dig did.
LEON		We would too have gone!
TAYLOR		*(laughing)* Look at him. Little dosser with his shirt out.
SOPH		Why's he stopped?
LEON		Oi, Big Ishoo, get on with it!
DIG		He's waiting to see if they come out of the playground.
SOPH		He's going nearer.
DIG		He's calling them. He doesn't want to go in the playground, it's harder to run away if you're in the playground.
MEL		They're coming.
DIG		No, they've stopped. They're staying by the fence.
TAYLOR		Scumbags don't want to come out of the playground.
LEON		They're shouting at him.
SOPH		He's going nearer.
DIG		*(shouts)* Don't go in the playground, Marky!
TAYLOR		He's stopped again.
LEON		Man, they ain't going to come out.
SOPH		Dig, tell him not to go in the playground.
DIG		*(shouts)* Marky! Don't go in the playground!
SOPH		I don't like this, this is bad. Dig, tell him it doesn't matter, tell him not to bother.
DIG		Marky, come back!

Soph jumps down from the bench, comes downstage.

SOPH   *(shouts)* Marky, it's all right! Don't bother!

LEON   He's by the fence now. He's talking to them.

DIG   Yeah, they're just talking.

TAYLOR   Big Ishoo, he'll talk em to death.

MEL   It's okay, it's going to be all right…

LEON   He's going in the playground…

DIG   *(quiet)* No! Marky!

Soph jumps back on the bench.

TAYLOR   Stay near the gate… *(shouts)* Stay near the gate!

DIG   *(shouts)* Stay near the gate!

TAYLOR   Marky!

LEON   The big geezer's got him!

TAYLOR   Give him one Marky!

Consternation on the benches.

LEON   That big geezer's got him!

DIG   Marky's fighting him!

TAYLOR   Hit the bastard, Marky!

DIG   He's got away!

TAYLOR   He's out the gate!

MEL   Run Marky!

TAYLOR   The geezer's chasing him!

MEL/SOPH   *(clinging to each other, shouting)* Run, run!

LEON	Behind you, Marky!

*Mel and **Soph** scream.*

DIG	No! Marky!

A beat or two of complete silence.

LEON	He's down…
DIG	He's… he's…
LEON	The big geezer hit him!
DIG	No…
TAYLOR	Get up, Marky!
DIG	No.
LEON	He hit him!
SOPH	No! He stabbed him!
DIG	No.
MEL	He stabbed him up!
DIG	No.
LEON	They're coming! They're coming after us!

*Everybody runs off in different directions except **Dig**. Still on the bench, peering into the distance.*

DIG	Marky! Marky, get up!
SOPH	*(off, screaming)* Dig!

***Dig** jumps off the bench and runs.*

Blackout. Off, a police siren wails.

Scene Two

Dig sits on the right-hand bench, slumped forward, staring at the ground between his feet. He will remain there throughout this scene, isolated from – and oblivious to – the action.

*A **Police Officer** in fluorescent yellow jacket stretches police tape across the stage. **Passers-by** line up behind the tape and gawp at the audience.*

*Two **Newsreaders** sit at either end of the left-hand bench as if in a studio. They fiddle with their hair, adjust ties, etc.*

*A **TV Reporter** with a mike stands by the police tape.*

NEWSREADER 1 Here is the news. Reports are coming in of an assault on a teenager in Albion Park.

NEWSREADER 2 ~~Here is the news.~~ A fourteen-year-old youth was murdered in Albion Park this morning. Early reports indicate that the killing took place during a fight between rival gangs.

NEWSREADER 1 The fourteen-year-old youth murdered in Albion Park has been named as Mark Bennett. He was a pupil at Albion Park School.

NEWSREADER 2 Reports suggest that the Mark Bennett, the murdered teenager, belonged to one of the gangs that have been terrorising Albion Park School.

NEWSREADER 1 Albion Park School, the school attended by Mark Bennett, has been criticised recently by government inspectors for its poor disciplinary record.

NEWSREADER 2 Parents say police were called to the school on a regular basis. They say a yob culture prevailed at the troubled secondary school.

TV REPORTER I'm in Albion Park, scene of the brutal murder of Mark Bennett, the fourteen-year-old pupil at nearby Albion Park School. Local residents say they are terrorised by the gangs which roam the park.

*The **TV Reporter** sticks the mike in the face of a **Gawper**.*

GAWPER 1   There's always trouble. Every day. Fights, muggings. You daren't go out the house.

*The **TV Reporter** sticks the mike in the face of another **Gawper**.*

GAWPER 2   It's the kids from the school. They hang around the benches and the playground, they never go to school, do they? They just hang around causing trouble.

*Gawper 2 is pushed out the way by **Gawper 3**.*

GAWPER 3   They attract undesirables. Druggies, winos. This used to be a nice area.

GAWPER 2   I mean, don't get me wrong, I'm sorry for what happened to the poor kid, but what can you expect? There's just no discipline, is there?

GAWPER 3   It was an accident waiting to happen. Somebody should've done something.

GAWPER 1   Nobody cares anymore, do they? People used to look after each other, now they just can't be bothered.

TV REPORTER   Police are asking for witnesses to come forward.

*The yellow-jacketed **Police Officer** approaches **Gawper 1** with a notebook.*

POLICE OFFICER   Did you see anything?

GAWPER 1   Me? I didn't see anything!

*Gawper 1 hurries off. The **Police Officer** approaches **Gawper 2**.*

POLICE OFFICER   Did you see anything?

GAWPER 2   Me? You're joking! I got better things to do than hang around here all day, haven't I?

*Gawper 2 hurries off. The **Police Officer** approaches **Gawper 3**.*

POLICE OFFICER Did you see anything?

GAWPER 3 Look at the time! Sorry, I got to go to work!

Gawper 3 hurries off.

*Exit everyone except **Dig**, still sitting on the bench.*

Blackout. Off, a police siren wails.

Scene Three

The benches. Police tape across the stage.

Dig *still sitting on the right-hand bench. Hunched over, staring at the ground in front of him.*

Soph *and* ***Mel*** *enter, walking slowly, supporting each other. Both holding bunches of flowers. They sit on the left-hand bench, put the flowers down on the bench beside them. Both have been crying. They huddle together, holding hands, clutching soggy tissues.*

After a bit, ***Soph*** *notices* ***Dig***. *She gets up, goes over to him.*

SOPH   Dig?

Dig *doesn't look up, doesn't answer.*

SOPH   You alright, Dig?

Dig *nods without looking up.* ***Soph*** *lingers, maybe reaches out a hand as if to touch him on the shoulder, then changes her mind and goes back to the left-hand bench, sits down next to* ***Mel***.

Beat.

SOPH   You see what they said on the news?

MEL   What?

SOPH   They said Marky was in a gang.

MEL   No!

SOPH   Can you believe it?

MEL   Marky in a gang? You're joking!

SOPH   I told him to come back! I told him not to bother! Didn't I, Mel?

MEL   Yeah, you did.

SOPH   *(crying)* Everyone's going to think it was my fault.

MEL   It wasn't your fault. Tell her, Dig!

No reply from **Dig**.

MEL   Oi, Dig! It wasn't her fault, was it?

No reply from **Dig**.

SOPH   Leave him.

Taylor enters, walks over to the left-hand bench to join **Mel** *and* **Soph**.

TAYLOR   School's closed.

MEL   We know.

TAYLOR   And tomorrow, probably.

Taylor sees the flowers on the bench.

TAYLOR   What's this?

MEL   We were going to put them over there, where
                    Marky was – you know.

TAYLOR   Best leave them on the bench. They'll get trashed
                    over by the playground.

MEL   Yeah, they're better here, aren't they? He was
                    always sat here, wasn't he?

SOPH   He was always on the benches, every morning.

MEL   Yeah, he was.

TAYLOR   And this was his favourite bench, right?

Nobody answers. **Taylor** *looks over at* **Dig**.

TAYLOR   You alright, Dig?

Dig doesn't answer.

36

MEL   Leave him.

Soph starts crying.

TAYLOR   Hey Soph.

Taylor tries to sit down on the bench but Mel pushes him away.

MEL   Leave us alone.

Mel puts her arms round Soph. Taylor goes and sits down next to Dig.

TAYLOR   I still can't believe it! *(beat, then to Dig)* Can you, Dig?

Dig doesn't answer.

TAYLOR   It's like a dream or something. Know what I mean?

Dig doesn't respond.

Leon enters. Goes over to Soph and Mel who are still clutching each other. Looks at them for a moment or two. Leon goes to the right-hand bench, climbs up, looks out over the park.

LEON   *(shouts)* Scumbags!

Leon jumps down, goes to the police tape, looks over it.

LEON   They show their faces round here again, they're dead meat!

TAYLOR   There's no one there, Leon. Just police.

LEON   Yeah, cops everywhere, man. I was stopped twice on the way here.

Beat.

                 Never see 'em for weeks then they're harassing you every five minutes.

TAYLOR	I was up at the school. I was talking to Mr Gillespie. He's well sick.
MEL	We all are, Tayl.
TAYLOR	He's well sick about what they said on the news about the school, and Marky being in a gang.
LEON	Worried about his job, that's what he's worried about.
SOPH	You didn't say anything about my mum's phone!
TAYLOR	Course not.
MEL	What were you doing at school anyway, if you knew it was closed?
TAYLOR	Just wanted to see what was going on, that's all.
LEON	Sucking up, that's what he was doing. 'Good morning, Mr Gillespie, anything I can do to help?'
TAYLOR	Watch your mouth, Leon.
SOPH	*(to Leon)* You can talk.
LEON	Oh right, now you're going to have a go at me, right?
SOPH	Yeah, 'cos you didn't help him! You let Marky go on his own!
TAYLOR	Marky didn't want us to go with him, remember? He said they'd run away if we all went.
SOPH	No, Tayl, you said that. *(to Leon)* And you.
LEON	No way!
MEL	He's right, Soph. Marky didn't want them to help.
SOPH	*(to Mel)* What is your problem? Always sticking up for these losers.
TAYLOR	*(to Soph)* Hey, you'd better be careful what you say, girl!

38

SOPH	Or what, Tayl? You going to sort me out like you did the muggers?
TAYLOR	No, I'm just saying, that's all.
SOPH	You're always just saying, Tayl, that's your problem. Your big mouth never stops flapping for one second!
TAYLOR	I'm just saying you've got to be careful when you talk to the police.
MEL	What do you mean?
TAYLOR	Mr Gillespie says we have to make statements to the police, at the police station.
LEON	No way!
TAYLOR	You have to have a parent with you…
LEON	No way!
TAYLOR	… there'll be counsellors, social workers, the lot. So what I'm saying is, you've got to be careful what you say.
SOPH	Don't say anything about my mum's phone!
MEL	Why not? Marky was trying to get it back, he was trying to help…
SOPH	*(tearful)* I haven't told her I took it. She thinks she left it in Tesco's. What if she finds out I took it, then got mugged, then Marky got stabbed up trying to get it back? I can't tell them that! My mum would go totally ape. Leon, you know what she's like – I can't tell her that, can I?
LEON	Well, we don't have to tell them about the phone, do we?
TAYLOR	That's what I'm saying. We've got to be careful. If they think Marky was in a gang, they'll think *we're* in a gang.

MEL	Joking!
TAYLOR	*They* were the gang, not us! That's what we tell them! There was a whole gang of them, right?

Dig stands. Agitated.

DIG	SHUT UP! Just – shut – up.

Silence.

DIG	We tell them what happened, that's what we do.
TAYLOR	Tell them what, Dig?
DIG	Tell them what happened! Tell them who did it! Tell them who stabbed Marky up!

Silence from the others.

TAYLOR	Yeah but, the thing is Dig, we don't really know, do we?
DIG	Marky recognised him! He recognised the big geezer! His mum lives next to Marky's mum. Marky said so. That's what we tell the police!
TAYLOR	*We* don't know he was, do we?
DIG	Marky said his name was Carl.
LEON	Carl? You sure? I thought it was Kyle.
TAYLOR	Clive, was it? I dunno.
MEL	I can't remember.
DIG	It was Carl! Soph, you remember!
SOPH	Marky wasn't sure, Dig. He said he wasn't sure.
DIG	Marky recognised him!
LEON	What if he was wrong?

DIG	He knew the geezer!
TAYLOR	Mel, if you saw the big geezer again, would you recognise him?
MEL	No way! All I saw was this big geezer in a hoodie.
LEON	What about you, Soph?
SOPH	I don't know, do I? He was grabbing me, he was grabbing my phone, I didn't have time to notice what he looked like!
LEON	We're not even sure what his name is, right?
DIG	It's Carl!
TAYLOR	Or Kyle.
MEL	Or Clive.
LEON	He knows where Marky's mum lives. His mum lives next to Marky's mum.
MEL	Yeah, that's true.
LEON	Think about that for one second, all right? We grass him up, he'll be straight over there, him and his mates. Then he'll be straight over here.
TAYLOR	What if we're wrong, what if we say something about this big geezer and we're wrong, it wasn't him, and they come over here and stab us up?
LEON	Stab *you* up Dig, if you say something!
TAYLOR	Yeah, and none of us can identify him anyway, so they'll have to let him go and he'll come straight here looking for us.
MEL	*(tearful)* I don't want to talk to the police, I'm too upset!
LEON	Well, we're all upset, aren't we? He was our mate too, wasn't he?
TAYLOR	Yeah, he was our mate, too.

*And **Dig**, wailing, launches himself at **Taylor** in a frenzied attack. Knocks **Taylor** to the floor. **Leon** manages to wrestle **Dig** off **Taylor** and restrain him, twisting his arm.*

TAYLOR	What's your problem?
DIG	He wasn't your mate!
TAYLOR	Course he was!
DIG	*(in pain)* Let me go!
LEON	You going to behave yourself?

***Dig** struggles but **Leon** is too strong for him.*

DIG	*(in pain, mumbling)* Yeah.

***Leon** shakes him.*

LEON	Are you?
DIG	*(louder)* Yes!
LEON	And when you talk to the cops?
DIG	Yes!
SOPH	Don't tell them about the phone, Dig, all right?
DIG	All right!
SOPH	Promise?
DIG	*(miserable)* Yeah, I promise!

***Leon** lets him go. **Dig** runs off.*

Blackout. Off, a police siren wails.

Scene Four

The police tape still across the stage. There are more flowers on the left-hand bench now.

Members of the public *and* **schoolkids** *file past, placing flowers and cards on the bench. Some pause to read the cards and messages. Some take photos with their mobile phones, some stop and hug each other.*

Meanwhile, **Newsreaders** *1 and 2 have settled at either end of the right-hand bench. They fiddle with their hair, adjust ties and so on.*

Newsreader 1 Here is the news. Police say that Mark Bennett, the schoolboy who was stabbed to death in Albion Park, may have been killed during an argument over a mobile phone.

Newsreader 2 Here is the news. Witnesses say that Mark Bennett was seen trying to grab a youth's mobile phone moments before he was stabbed to death.

Newsreader 1 Reports are emerging that Mark Bennett was carrying a knife at the time of his death.

Newsreader 2 Police emphasise that the knife found on Mark Bennett's body was not the murder weapon.

Newsreader 1 Mark Bennett had been suspended from school on a number of occasions for poor attendance and disruptive behaviour.

Newsreader 2 Police say they are having trouble getting pupils at Albion Park School to make statements because of the widespread fear of retribution.

Newsreader 1 In a recent survey, one in four children aged between eleven and sixteen claim to have carried knives.

The **Newsreaders** *get up and leave, the last of the* **Passers-by** *file out.*

Dig *enters, walks over to the left-hand bench, checks out the flowers. He looks around to make sure nobody is watching, then takes a small, scruffy bunch of flowers from inside his coat.*

Soph enters from the other side. Dig sees her, shoves the flowers back inside his coat.

Soph sits at one end of the right-hand bench. Dig hesitates, then goes to sit at the other end.

Beat.

DIG	I didn't tell them about your mum's phone.
SOPH	Thanks, Dig.

Beat.

SOPH	Did you tell them about the big geezer?
DIG	No.
SOPH	Me neither. I said I couldn't see anything, it was too far away.
DIG	Me too.

Beat.

SOPH	We couldn't see who it was, could we?
DIG	No.
SOPH	Even Marky wasn't sure, was he?

Dig doesn't answer. Then Mel, Leon and Taylor enter, all outrage and indignation, talking over each other.

TAYLOR	Can you believe it…
MEL	They want to make out it was *his* fault he got killed…
LEON	They're having a laugh, right…
MEL	It's all lies…
TAYLOR	It's a joke…

44

MEL	They lie all the time…
TAYLOR	Specially the telly…
MEL	Never mind the telly, did you see the paper…
LEON	It's that scumbag Gillespie…
MEL	They lie to make themselves look better…
TAYLOR	They lie 'cos people want them to…
LEON	If I find out it was Gillespie, I'm going to have him!
TAYLOR	*(to **Soph** and **Dig**)* Here, you see the news?
SOPH/DIG	No.
LEON	They're only saying Marky had a knife on him!
SOPH	A knife?
MEL	First they say he was in a gang, now they say he had a knife!
SOPH	Marky had a knife? You're joking!
LEON	That's what they said on the news.
SOPH	Who said?
LEON	That toerag teacher…
TAYLOR	Mr Gillespie wouldn't say that…
LEON	*(scornful)* 'Mister Gillespie'. Yeah, your little mate…
TAYLOR	Mr Gillespie wouldn't say that because it makes the school look bad! It's politics, Leon!
MEL	They said it to make *us* look bad.
SOPH	Who? Who said it?
TAYLOR	The police, the telly, everyone. The media, right? We're all bad, aren't we, all the kids at the school, all the kids in the park, it's easier for them if they make out we're all bad…

Soph	A knife? You sure, Leon?
Leon	Yeah, it was in his bag.
Taylor	*(to **Dig**)* You're very quiet.

*During the above, **Dig** has remained motionless, staring at the ground between his feet.*

Dig	So?
Taylor	Know anything about Marky having a knife?
Dig	No.
Soph	Marky never had a knife, Tayl!
Taylor	*(looking at **Dig**)* Maybe he did.
Mel	No way!
Taylor	Maybe he nicked it.
Leon	Yeah, Marky nicked stuff, didn't he, Dig?
Taylor	Him and Dig were always nicking stuff. Eh, Dig?
Dig	No!
Taylor	*(to **Dig**)* I've seen you two, sitting on the benches, showing each other stuff you've nicked.
Mel	Marky only nicked fags and sweets.

***Leon** and **Taylor** are now standing over **Dig**, menacing him.*

Taylor	Yeah, right! So where'd you get the fags you gave Soph?
Dig	I bought them.
Taylor	Joking!
Leon	He got the fags off Marky, didn't he?
Taylor	You nicked the knife, didn't you, Dig? You nicked the knife and swapped it for fags!

Dig	No, I didn't!
Leon	If you did man, you'd better tell the cops.
Dig	Well, I didn't!
Soph	Come on, Leon, Dig wouldn't steal a knife…
Leon	What would you know about it? If you hadn't nicked your mum's phone this wouldn't have happened…

Soph jumps to her feet.

Soph	Don't say that!
Leon	Sit down…

Leon shoves Soph back down onto the bench. Dig stands, confronts Leon.

Dig	Don't touch her!
Leon	*(laughing)* Or what?
Taylor	You going going to tell them about the knife, you thieving little dosser?
Dig	Just stop it, Tayl, all right?
Taylor	What? Stop what?
Dig	Stop making stuff up!
Taylor	*(to Leon)* What's he on about?
Leon	No idea.
Dig	Making stuff up about Marky, just to make yourself feel better! Stuff about being his mate! Stuff about his favourite bench. It's a joke! Whatever bench we sat on, you chucked us off it! Maybe I'll tell them about that.
Taylor	What, you'll tell the cops about me chucking you off the benches? I'm sure they'll be fascinated.

DIG	I'll tell them how you called Marky Big Ishoo and Dosser, and I'll them how Leon beat us up and took our money, and I'll tell them about that time me and Marky got mugged and the muggers beat us up 'cos we didn't have any money 'cos you two mugged us first…

Leon hits Dig hard in the face. Soph screams. Dig collapses back on the bench. Leon straddles him, hits him again.

LEON	Don't even think about it!

Soph starts trying to drag Leon off.

SOPH	Get off him, Leon!

Leon allows himself to be pulled off Dig. Dig lies in a heap on the bench. Taylor leans over him.

TAYLOR	Nobody cares about any of that, Dig. Don't you get it? That's not on the agenda right now.
MEL	Is he all right?
TAYLOR	Yeah, he's all right.
LEON	He won't be if he tells the cops any of that crap.
SOPH	*(examining Dig)* You pig, you really hurt him!
LEON	Good.
SOPH	Dig, you okay?

Dig struggles upright, a hand over his nose. Maybe some blood. Nods.

TAYLOR	Yeah, he's all right. Come on, let's go. Mel, you coming?
MEL	Yeah, I s'pose.
LEON	*(to Dig)* Keep it buttoned, dosser.
TAYLOR	Come on, Leon, let's go.

48

LEON	Come on, Soph. We're going.
SOPH	I'm staying here.
TAYLOR	He's all right, Soph.
LEON	Come on, girl! *Now!*
SOPH	I said I'm staying here.

Beat. **Leon** *looks menacing.*

SOPH	What're you doing to do? Hit me as well, you pig?
LEON	*(suddenly unsure of himself)* So I'll see you later, all right?
SOPH	I don't think so.
LEON	I said, I'll see you later, all right?
SOPH	I said, I don't think so!

Beat.

| LEON | All right, stay with the loser if that's what you want. |

Leon, **Mel** *and* **Taylor** *exit.* **Leon** *pausing for a final look back at* **Soph**. *She ignores him.* **Soph** *and* **Dig** *sit side by side on the left-hand bench.* **Soph** *fumbles in her pocket.*

SOPH	You want a tissue?
DIG	I'm not crying. My eyes are watering 'cos he hit my nose.
SOPH	I know.

Soph *finds a tissue in her bag, hands it to* **Dig**.

| DIG | Ta. |

Dig *mops his nose.*

Dig	Marky had a theory about Leon.
Soph	What was that?
Dig	Marky said Leon beat us up because he was scared.
Soph	Yeah?
Dig	I didn't get it. I still don't.
Soph	Marky's right. Leon's scared of everything.
Dig	Nah!
Soph	He was scared of the big geezer, wasn't he?

Dig considers this.

Dig	Yeah, he was, wasn't he? He wouldn't go with Marky, would he?
Soph	No.
Dig	He made excuses. You could tell he was scared.
Soph	Yeah, he was scared. We all were.
Dig	Yes.

Beat.

Dig	Soph?
Soph	What?
Dig	About the knife.
Soph	What about it?

Beat.

Dig	I nicked it.
Soph	I know.
Dig	You know?

Soph	Well, I guessed. I got here before the others that morning. I was down there, texting Leon. I saw you and Marky shoving stuff back in your bags. Then Mel and Tayl turned up.

Beat.

Dig	I got it from the art shop. I was after felt-tips but the bloke in there, he's such a suspicious bastard, always looking at you like you're going to do something, but he had to answer the phone so I just grabbed the box and ran. I wasn't after a knife at all, I was after felt-tips.

Beat.

I made Marky swap it for fags so I could give them to you.

Beat.

Why didn't you tell the others?

Soph	You didn't tell the police about my mum's phone.

Beat.

Dig	How do you tell the truth? About what actually happened? You know, tell the *actual* truth. It's all so complicated.
Soph	I bet Marky had a theory about it.
Dig	Yeah, probably.

Dig remembers something. Stands, takes the bedraggled flowers out from inside his coat. Even more bedraggled now. He goes over to the left-hand bench, looks at the flowers on the bench, then at the pathetic offering he's holding in his hand. Chucks them in the bin.

Dig	I'm going to tell them about the knife, Soph.

SOPH	Are you, Dig?
DIG	Yeah. And the big geezer.
SOPH	I think that's great.
DIG	You do?
SOPH	Yeah, I do. I think that's really great, Dig.

Beat.

SOPH	I'll come with you.
DIG	Really?
SOPH	Yeah. You can tell them about the knife and I'll tell them about my mum's phone.

Blackout.

Scene Five

The police tape still in place. More flowers on the left-hand bench. **Gawpers**, *including* **Gawpers 1**, **2** *and* **3**, *stand around peering at the flowers, trying to read the cards.*

The **TV Reporter** *also stands beside the left-hand bench with* **Taylor**, **Leon** *and* **Mel**. *Also fiddling with their hair, straightening ties.*

Newsreaders 1 *and* **2** *sit on the right-hand bench as if in TV studio. The usual hair adjustments and so on.*

NEWSREADER 1   Here is the news. Police investigating the murder of Albion Park schoolboy Mark Bennett say they have uncovered important new evidence.

NEWSREADER 2   Police say a witness has come forward who may be able to identify the killer of Mark Bennett.

NEWSREADER 1   New evidence suggests that Mark was trying to retrieve a mobile phone which had been stolen from a friend.

NEWSREADER 2   Witnesses also say the knife found in Mark Bennett's bag belonged to another friend.

NEWSREADER 1   Mark, who feared the knife might get his school friend into trouble, had persuaded the friend to give it to him for safe-keeping.

NEWSREADER 2   Earlier reports that Mark Bennett's murder was gang-related may have been inaccurate. We're now going over to our roving reporter.

TV REPORTER   I'm in Albion Park, scene of the tragic murder of Mark Bennett, where I'm talking to some of his friends.

The **TV Reporter** *turns to* **Taylor**, **Leon** *and* **Mel**.

Can you tell me what your feelings are at this moment?

*The **TV Reporter** holds the mike to the three friends.*

TAYLOR Devastated. The whole school is in shock.

LEON We're gutted.

TV REPORTER You were friends of Mark, weren't you?

MEL/TAYLOR/ *(speaking at the same time)* Yeah/Yeah, he was a
LEON really good friend/a great mate/Mark was
brilliant/everybody liked Mark.

TV REPORTER It seems that Mark may have been trying to help
the victim of a mugging. Was that typical of Mark,
would you say?

TAYLOR Yeah, I'd say that was very typical of Mark. He was
very concerned about the situation here in the park,
with young kids getting mugged everyday…

MEL … they're afraid to go across the park, right, 'cos
that's where the muggers are…

TAYLOR In fact, sometimes kids are too scared to go to
school at all. They come to the park and if the
muggers are here, they just go home again which is
a totally unacceptable situation, right?

LEON Totally unacceptable.

TAYLOR Mark used to talk about this a lot, he used to talk
about organising something, right, to help the little
kids. He could've done it too, he was really clever.

LEON Mark was brilliant, he was going to get As in all his
GCSEs, definitely…

TAYLOR Anyway, we're going to talk to Mr Gillespie the
headteacher and the parents about setting up a
trust, the Mark Bennett Trust right, to help the
victims of muggings, like young kids…

LEON There's going to be a hotline…

MEL … for young kids to phone up if they're scared.

TAYLOR	So something good may come out of this terrible tragedy. Something that will make everyone remember Mark.

Blackout.

Scene Six

Taylor, Leon and Mel have exited. The Newsreaders and the Gawpers remain, as in Scene Five.

NEWSREADER 1 I'm sorry to have to cut you off there, but there is some breaking news. Police have arrested a twenty-year-old man in connection with the murder of Mark Bennett, star pupil of Albion Park School.

NEWSREADER 2 Friends of Mark Bennett say that Mark frequently voiced his concern about violent crime in the Albion Park area.

NEWSREADER 1 Mark Bennett's headteacher, David Gillespie, said that Mark's attitude showed great social awareness for his age. This was something that he and his colleagues at Albion Park School always encouraged.

NEWSREADER 2 Mr Gillespie said that he had already picked Mark out as a potential university entrant. We can now rejoin our reporter.

The TV Reporter is now beside the Gawpers.

TV REPORTER This is Albion Park, scene of the brutal murder of Mark Bennett, the brilliant young pupil at Albion Park School. As you can see, people are still coming here in droves to pay their respects. Excuse me, did you know Mark Bennett?

The TV Reporter shoves the mike at the Gawpers.

GAWPER 1 Oh yes, he was a lovely young lad.

GAWPER 2 He was always full of fun…

GAWPER 3 Like they said on the news, he was always trying to help…

GAWPER 1 Nothing was too much trouble for him…

GAWPER 2   Course, I didn't know him myself, but I know people who did…

GAWPER 3   I'd see him around the park, he'd always say hello…

GAWPER 1   Always smiling…

GAWPER 3   He was a lovely boy…

GAWPER 2   And clever with it, you know.

GAWPER 1   He could've done anything…

GAWPER 3   He had his whole life ahead of him.

*Everyone exits except **Newsreader 1**.*

NEWSREADER 1   There will be a memorial service for Mark Bennett at St Mary's Church on Thursday.

Newsreader 1 *exits.*

Blackout.

Scene Seven

The police tape has gone. The left-hand bench is still covered in flowers.

Dig enters. He pauses to check out the flowers. Dig looks different. The changes are slight – perhaps his hair is tidier, or his clothes tidier – but he looks older, more self-assured. Dig goes over to the right-hand bench and sits.

Taylor, Leon and Mel enter.

TAYLOR Alright, Dig?

DIG Alright.

They go over to join Dig on the right-hand bench.

TAYLOR They arrested that big geezer then. Carl.

DIG Yeah, they did.

LEON Scumbag.

TAYLOR You told the police, did you, Dig?

DIG I just told them what Marky said. So they arrested the geezer, then Soph went and identified him. She said it was easy, she recognised him straight away.

MEL I was going to go, right, and say something but they already arrested him, so there wasn't much point.

LEON You need a bit of time, right, after seeing something like that.

TAYLOR It's the shock, you can't remember every little detail straight away, can you?

Beat.

DIG I s'pose not.

Beat.

TAYLOR	You see what they're saying about Marky on the telly?
DIG	About him being a brilliant student?
TAYLOR	That was Leon's fault, saying he was going to get As.
LEON	I was trying to be nice, wasn't I?
DIG	Marky's 'social awareness', what's that about?
MEL	Well, he worried about getting mugged, didn't he?
DIG	Oh, that's what it means.
TAYLOR	Mr Gillespie was well pleased. He said 'Thank God someone's saying something positive about the school for once'.
DIG	*(mild)* Pity none of it's true.
TAYLOR	Dig, man, it's better than what they were saying before, isn't it? About Marky being in a gang and crap like that?
DIG	It's politics, right Tayl?
TAYLOR	Exactly. And there's going to be the Mark Bennett Trust…
MEL	And a hotline…
TAYLOR	And the council are going to put a new bench there…

Taylor points at the left-hand bench.

LEON	… with Marky's name on it.
DIG	*(amused rather than angry)* His favourite bench, right Tayl?
TAYLOR	We can't put his name on a bit of mud in the middle of the park, can we?
DIG	I s'pose not.

TAYLOR	Anyway, Mr Gillespie was looking for you. He was asking, did you want to say something at the Memorial Service?
DIG	Me?
LEON	You were his mate, weren't you?

Dig ponders.

DIG	No, I don't think I could do that.
TAYLOR	Okay, but you're going to come.
DIG	Course I am.
TAYLOR	Okay, then, we'll see you there.

Taylor, Mel and Leon exit. Leon stops.

LEON	Hey Dig.
DIG	Yeah?
LEON	You seen Soph?
DIG	I'm meeting her later.
LEON	She all right then?
DIG	Yeah, she's all right.
LEON	Right. So she's all right then.
DIG	Yeah.
LEON	Dig, man. I was going to say…
DIG	What?
LEON	About some of the stuff that happened before… *(tails off)*
DIG	Don't worry about it, Leon.
LEON	Right. Okay. Later, yeah?

DIG   Yeah, later.

Leon, relieved, exits.

DIG   Dazzling repartee.

Blackout.

Scene Eight

*Flowers still piled on the left-hand bench. A blow-up of a fuzzy colour snap of **Marky** hangs over the stage.*

*Everyone, including **Dig**, **Soph**, **Taylor**, **Leon** and **Mel**, is on-stage, backs to the audience, facing the right-hand bench.*

*A **Vicar** climbs on the right-hand bench to address them. Perhaps some organ music or a suggestion of light through stained glass.*

VICAR   Friends, we are here today to celebrate the life of Mark Bennett who was so tragically taken from us. I'm sure there is no one here whose life was not touched in some way by this remarkable young man, this young man of such exceptional gifts and talents. Some of you, particularly the younger ones, might be asking 'What are we doing here, in this church? Our friend Mark, our "best mate", has been taken from us. How is coming here going to help us in this dark hour?' Well, let me tell you: God, and his son Jesus, can be a great help at times like this, they can help 'big time', if you'll only let them…

***Dig** turns to face the audience. He's holding a giant milkshake. (The straw and container are mostly white – no logo.) The **Vicar** continues to address the congregation (silently) as **Dig** talks.*

DIG   I suppose God had to get in on the act sooner or later. Well, why not, everybody else has. It's funny… Marky had this theory, right, that if you really wanted something, you only got it when you stopped wanting it. He got this theory because of his dad. Marky's dad was supposed to come and take him out every Saturday and but he was always late or he'd never turn up, and Marky used to lie awake all Friday night worrying about whether his dad was going to turn up or not. And one night Marky thought 'Right, game over. I don't care anymore' and went to sleep and the next day his dad turned up, bang on time, with a wicked present. So that's that where that theory came from, and I didn't really get it, but I think I do now. Marky always wanted to do well at school – without having to do any work, right – and suddenly he's this brilliant student who was going to get As in everything and go to university. And Marky always wanted to be famous, and now he's famous. And he wanted lots of friends – 'It's important to have a social life, Dig' he used to say…

A beat while **Dig** *composes himself.*

Dig   … and now he's got all these new friends, people who ignored him or treated him like dirt or didn't even know him in the first place, but it isn't much good to him now, is it? So maybe that theory is rubbish.

Beat.

Dig   Or maybe that's the whole point of it.

Vicar   Let us pray.

The **Congregation** *lower their heads.*

Vicar   Dear father in heaven…

The **Vicar** *leads them in prayer (silently) as* **Dig** *continues talking to the audience.*

Dig   Anyway. All the things that have been said about Marky, the good things, the bad things, they're all about someone else, this person called 'Mark Bennett', they're not about Marky. Nobody seems to mind that, but I do, 'cos I want to remember him properly.

Beat.

What I want to remember is that Marky was my best friend. He was funny. He invented weird drinks. He never did any work. He was brilliant at nicking sweets. He once wore the same shirt for two weeks. He had a theory about everything. He told the truth, not all the time, but more than anybody else I know. And he was very brave. That's what Marky was really like. And I'll never forget him.

EVERYONE   Amen.

*The **Vicar** makes the sign of the cross over the **Congregation** and everyone except **Soph** and **Dig** files off silently.*

***Dig** goes over to the left-hand bench and carefully places the milkshake among the flowers. **Soph** joins him. They stand side by side looking at flowers for a beat or two.*

SOPH   We'd better go.

DIG   Okay.

SOPH   Do you want to go round or across?

DIG   Let's go across.

They join hands and walk off. FADE OUT TO BLACK, leaving the milkshake till last.

End.

Staging the play

Andrew Payne has specified that there must be two benches on the set. He suggests that one bench is what is known in theatre as DSR (down-stage right) and the other DSL (down-stage left). These terms refer to two areas on a proscenium arched, or end-on, stage. Left and right is from the *actor's* point of view (when looking at the audience). However, bear in mind when reading the play that Andrew Payne's directions are from the audience's perspective.

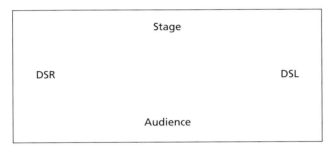

Your acting area could either be raised up on blocks or it could be the flat floor of the studio. This will depend on whether or not the audience is raised on terraced seating. If they are, it may be possible to perform on the floor of the drama studio – a flat stage area. If not, you may have to raise the acting area so that people sitting towards the back can see, particularly as there is quite a lot of sitting down in this play.

Finding places on-stage

On nine large pieces of cardboard, write the names of the following positions: 'Centre-stage', 'Up-stage', 'Down-stage', 'Down-stage right', 'Down-stage left', 'Up-stage right', 'Up-stage eft', 'Mid-stage right' and 'Mid-stage left'.

Then, with your class, label these nine areas with the pieces of card. When that is done, ask a group member to shout out randomly the names of these nine areas, and everyone should run to them as quickly as they can and stand there.

Physical warm-up

Another exercise which will motivate the group to work together physically is to have them walk slowly around the room. The leader then shouts out two numbers: the first is the number of people they should get themselves into groups of; and the second is the number of points of contact they may have with the floor. Encourage the actors to be inventive in the shapes they create. So, for example, for a group of 30 actors, the leader could shout out "5 and 3!" Everyone would then have to rush into groups of five and work out a way of having only three points of contact with the floor. The first group to achieve this is the winner. Repeat the exercise several times, being more ambitious each time. Another benefit of doing this exercise is that the actors will break any barriers they have about having physical contact with each other: when the game is played fast, there is no time to think or have inhibitions.

Rehearsing

Using coloured sticky tape, mark out on the floor where any props, such as benches, are going to be so that you know where everything is as you rehearse. Also, if you can't use the props you will use during the play, try to use something similar, for example, chairs without arms. Work in a space the same size as the stage or acting studio where your performance will take place. Ideally, it should be as uncluttered as possible to give the impression of the wide open outdoor space the play takes place in.

 SET

Andrew Payne has set the entire play on an open space called Albion Park. He got the idea for the location from Highbury Fields in North London, though, of course, the play is written so that it can be set anywhere and the characters could come from any region. Look at the photograph of Highbury Fields on the next page, so you can get a visual idea of the writer's starting point for the story.

Highbury Fields, North London

Highbury Fields is a few acres of rough grassland surrounded by houses. It is where local people go to walk their dogs, play ball games, sunbathe in summer and build snowmen in winter. In good weather it is a very pretty green area in the middle of a dense urban landscape. In cold weather it can look quite bleak, and this may be due in part to its flatness and emptiness. It is possible to stand on one side of the field and not quite be able to see the whole distance across to the other side, due to trees obscuring the sightlines or, on a particularly cold day, due to the mist that can settle in these open areas. The place also has a sense of foreboding about it because it's a very open space surrounded by a heavily built-up residential area. The openness of Highbury Fields can be enjoyed by people wanting to escape the claustrophobia of their small flats and houses, though it can also, especially when it is growing dark, be quite an intimidating and eerie place.

Activity — Preparing for the scene

Think of an open space near your school which is similar to Highbury Fields and see if you can arrange for your class to go there. If the whole class can't go, ask someone to go and take photographs that you can put on your drama studio wall as a visual starting point for imagining Albion Park Open Space. The key to getting the overall design of the acting space right is ensuring that the audience can imagine that they are seeing a small part of a much larger space.

You should give some consideration to the choice of backcloth you are going to use, but avoid a realistic-looking skyscape. One option is to use a matt black background, which will enable you to create a psychological sense of darkness and danger and, with use of back-lighting (lights rigged up-stage of the action, pointing towards the actors giving them a halo effect), you will be able to suggest the distance of the park.

Entrances and exits are very important in this play. The curtains or pieces of scenery on each side of the stage from behind which the actors appear when making their entrances are known as masking. Make sure that this is neat and hides all off-stage areas so that the actors are able to make clean exits and entrances, which don't delay the dialogue or action.

Some of the entrances are quite powerful, for example, when Soph arrives immediately after her mobile phone has been stolen. The actors need to arrive immediately into the focus of the acting area without having to walk great distances to get to it. As the play is set outdoors, the convention when people walk on is that they have been travelling on-foot for some time before we see them, unlike other plays where they enter through doors which are part of the story of the set. That is why you should go to some trouble to ensure that the masking on each side of your acting area is neutral and serves the actors well by enabling them to make swift, uncomplicated entrances. Avoid them having to part curtains to get on-stage, for example, as this kills the impression that the audience is seeing the last part of a lengthy walk as the characters arrive in the acting space where the story is unfolding. They should enter through unblocked spaces in the masking.

The two benches you use could be borrowed from your school playground, or even the local council. They should look like outdoor benches, and be stable and strong enough to withstand the weight of at least two actors standing on them. It may be necessary to screw them into the stage floor so that they don't move or topple when actors jump up on them. Don't worry if you can't find two identical benches, as parks often have benches which have been placed there at different times over many years. However, they must look as if they both exist in the same urban parkland, and in character they should be very sombre and fatigued, through many years of providing service.

The bin, which is situated near to one of the benches, should be so insignificant it is barely noticeable. It serves only to tell the story; it is not an important feature of the set. Bins in parks are often black, dark grey or green so that they don't pull focus from the natural colours of grass, plants and trees that visitors want to see. The sign which says 'Albion Park Open Space' should also be placed well off-centre and in a space which does not dominate the acting area; it should lose itself in the shadows. Once it has done the job of informing the audience of where they are it serves no further purpose. You could have it designed in very dull colours and break it down (which is a theatrical term for distressing costumes and props so that they don't look new) or, as the writer suggests in his introduction, cover it with graffiti so that it is only just legible.

COSTUMES AND PERSONAL PROPS

Everyone wears everyday contemporary clothes in this play so you should find it quite easy to costume. The kids wear school uniform. If your school has a uniform, don't use your own. You need to place the world of the play somewhere else. Phone a school uniform supplier to see if they have seconds of a certain type of tie – the rest of the uniform, white or grey blouses and shirts, trousers and skirts you can make up yourself. You may find that another local school has six school ties lying in their lost property box which they may lend you for your production. Each character should find a personalised way of wearing their school uniform!

As the play takes place outdoors in chilly weather, it is likely that all of the teenagers would wear coats. This gets around the problem of finding school blazers. They could wear an assortment of hoodies, fleeces, anoraks and ski-jackets. Choose whatever you think each character would wear. The actors playing those characters might have a personal choice that they would like to make about their costumes.

Personal props are small items carried on-stage by actors. They may wear them, like wristwatches, or carry them in their pockets or bags.

Planning props

Draw a table like the one below and then go through the script, carefully noting all the small personal props which are needed for a performance of *Mugged*.

When you have completed this list you will know who needs what and when they need it. You should then make a far more detailed list to give to your stage management team. This list should explain where each prop needs to be before the performance begins, and each actor should have the responsibility checking his or her own props. A second member of the stage management team should also check the props are all in place and tick them off on the list. This is a play in which it is crucial that all actors have the right props at the right time.

| | Scenes | | | | | | | |
	1	2	3	4	5	6	7	8
DIG	art knife							
MARKY	cigarettes (Marlboro)							
SOPH	mobile phone watch		mobile phone					
MEL			tissue					
TAYLOR								
LEON								

Don't stereotype the characters of the Gawpers. They could look just as aggressive as the members of the gang. They should be fully rounded characterisations, who the audience believe are genuinely caught up in the events, and they don't have to be that much older than the teenagers themselves. It would be a mistake to play the Gawpers for comedy.

LIGHTING

The most exciting moments for lighting effects are the scene transitions and the sequences when the news reporters appear.

It is worth phoning your local police station to ask if they have a spare blue light they are not using – as they may well have an old one that they have taken off a car – and there is nothing quite like using the real thing. Ask a Science teacher to wire it up to a 12-volt transformer so that you can switch it on and off with ease. Placed somewhere just off-stage so that there is maximum light spill across the set, it will generate a good effect of the police presence following the crime. Flashing emergency lights can be bought from joke shops, but the bulbs in them are very low wattage and not really bright enough for theatrical use. Alternatively, you can use an ordinary stage light with a blue gel in front and flash it on and off, though the effect is not quite the same as the police lights that appear to revolve as they use a mirror on a low-speed motor.

If you have the equipment, the news reporting could be done through a montage of prerecorded sound and video projection, and live action.

Work on and around the script

(B) LANGUAGE

There are two types of language used by the characters in *Mugged*: the direct and localised speech of the gang, and the formalised standard English of the Newsreaders.

> ## Writing
>
> Write the story of Marky's murder from three perspectives:
>
> **1.** A formal police report
>
> **2.** A tabloid newspaper
>
> **3.** Soph's private diary
>
> Consider the different elements that each form of writing would require.

(B)(S) SPOKEN LANGUAGE

The language spoken by the teenage characters is spare and they rarely complete sentences. They use one word when one word will do. You must be always aware when rehearsing that what each actor is doing physically on-stage at any time is as important as what they're saying.

BODY LANGUAGE

It should be clear at the start of the play, for example, that Dig and Marky are good friends. Even before either of them speak, their body language and the ease with which they eat the crisps and drink the milkshake should indicate this. Even when out of focus and not speaking, actors must continually be aware that their body language is still talking and telling the audience the story.

☞ DIVIDING UP THE PLAY

One of the first things you should do is to divide the scenes into units. A unit often starts and ends when a character arrives or leaves, or it could be a shift in subject matter in the characters' conversation. Units will be of various lengths. When you have divided the play into units you will find it easier to find the shape and pace of each section. Decide who is the dominant character in each unit: Who takes the lead in the dialogue? Where is the tension? What is the aim of each character? How does a character's arrival change the temperature of a scene, for example, Leon's arrival in Scene Three?

Identifying units

Here are two examples of units from Scene Three which follow each other. What is the main subject of Unit 1 and what does the subject change to in Unit 2?

Unit 1

TAYLOR   What's this?

MEL   We were going to put them over there, where Marky was – you know.

TAYLOR   Best leave them on the bench. They'll get trashed over by the playground.

MEL   Yeah, they're better here, aren't they? He was always sat here, wasn't he?

SOPH   He was always on the benches, every morning.

MEL   Yeah, he was.

TAYLOR   And this was his favourite bench, right?

*Nobody answers. **Taylor** looks over at **Dig**.*

Unit 2

TAYLOR   You alright, Dig?

***Dig** doesn't answer.*

MEL   Leave him.

How do the characters change from one scene to the next?

Each actor playing the six main characters should make a chart which illustrates his or her emotional journey. It would be useful if each actor wrote on the chart as many words as they could think of to describe the way in which their character responds to the murder.

When the characters leave the stage at the end of Scene One, they should stay in character all the way through Scene Two until they come on-stage again for Scene Three. This will help them to make the emotional leap into anger, shock and grief that we see in the third scene. They should leave the stage and sit quietly in the wings, completely ignoring anyone or anything around them, and listen to the actors playing the Newsreaders as if they are hearing the story for the first time. They should go through the journey off-stage during Scene Two, so that they are ready to play the heightened emotional states the characters need to be in in Scene Three.

Improvisation: A week before

Early in your rehearsal process, once casting is complete and people have had time to find their characters, it is worth imagining a day by the benches one week before the play takes place. The advantages of spending time off from the script are in the strengths your characters will gain, both as individuals and also in relationship to each other.

All six characters should be there and they should play a scene for a maximum of five minutes. Nothing particularly exciting has to happen; in a way, the more boring the scene is the better. All six actors need to take this opportunity to allow their imaginations to go to the world of those six characters by those two benches, so that everyone has an aural, visual and emotional reference to a typical school day spent hanging around the park.

Explore the dynamics between the characters, staying completely in character. See how far Taylor can push the girls; how far Soph can challenge Leon. When you've finished improvising, discuss any discoveries you have made by exploring characters and their relationships to each other whilst off-text.

Discovering the families

Improvise a scene in a small group. One of you should play one of the six teenagers from the play and everyone else takes a role as a member of his or her family. You should imagine the scene inside the family house when news breaks on local television or radio about the murder. How do the members of the family react? How does their son or daughter explain their involvement in the crime?

Newsreaders

The characters of the newsreaders should contrast with the teenagers. They should speak in very measured tones. They read the news every day and they always sound the same, whether they are reading news of great joy or tragedy. Watch television news programmes and try imitating their vocal tones and body language.

Hot-seating: Police interview

As a whole group, examine each character's actions leading up to the murder. Each one of them played a part in Marky's death.

When you have made a list, hot-seat the six main characters by asking them questions in the style of a police investigation interview.

♻ PLAYING INTENTION

Mugged uses a very simple plot to tell a complicated story. The characters are continually in a state of flux. They are often changing their opinions and allegiances, and what they say can sometimes have two or three contrasting meanings or objectives simultaneously.

Explore individual lines closely, for example, the line of Soph's to Dig and Mel in Scene Three: "I told him to come back! I told him not to bother! Didn't I Mel?" In that line she expresses guilt, grief, loss and fear of blame, and asks her friend for back-up. The actor playing Soph needs to find a way of playing all of these emotions at the same time through the line.

Taylor and Leon want to keep up their high status images, even after the murder, so they use hard-edged words like 'trashed' and 'right', whilst the girls are using more obviously sympathetic and gentle language. The boys playing these parts must find a way to let their vulnerability in this new circumstance bleed through their forced bravura.

FIGHTING AND FLIRTING

There is a thin line between fighting and flirting amongst this group of young people, which could also be explored through improvisation. Something that starts as playful can suddenly turn genuinely violent.

It is key that the director makes sure that the reactions of the rest of the group are true to the mood at any moment and reflect the shift from playfulness to threat.

In addition, you need to take great care when rehearsing the combat in the play. Each move should be meticulously planned. There should be no danger of real injury. The actors should know exactly what is going to happen and then perform each sequence of violence as if it is happening for the first time. For example:

Leon *manages to wrestle* **Dig** *off* **Taylor** *and restrain him, twisting his arm.* (Scene Three)

his arm there. Both actors then imitate the opposite of what is happening. So the actor playing Leon appears to be in control, whereas in fact the actor playing Dig is completely in control of his own restraint.

Stage combat

When Leon punches Dig in the face, he should use three distinct movements. They should happen so quickly the audience is not aware of the technique.

Firstly, Leon stretches his arm out to measure the distance between himself and the area just in front of Dig's face. He then pulls back and makes a fist. Thirdly, he makes the punch. As long as the actor playing Dig doesn't move he will be quite safe, as Leon can only punch the area in front of his face and shouldn't make any actual contact. Once this process has been rehearsed thoroughly, the two actors can add the acting which makes us believe that Dig has been hit. During this sequence, Dig should be up-stage of Leon, so the audience can't see the gap between the fist and the face.

Blood capsules can be bought from joke shops and stage make-up suppliers. The actor playing Dig could keep one in a pocket until the moment in Scene Three when he has been hit, and discreetly burst the capsule in his hand as he holds his hand over his face. If you want to avoid using wet fluids that might stain costumes for future performances, however, you could give Dig a tissue which has bright red blood-coloured paint on, which looks wet but is in fact dry.

Remember also, during fight sequences, the reactions of the onlookers are as important in creating realistic violence as the actions of the main characters pulling the punches.

Playing thought processes

Take a look at the end of Scene Three. At this point there is a significant sequence of action in which Dig remembers the flowers he has brought and decides to put them in the bin. It is at this moment that he decides

cont...

to tell the truth about the knife to the police. The actor playing Dig should talk through his entire thought process during this sequence in rehearsals so that when he plays the scene he has a 'step-by-step' thought process to go through before he puts the flowers in the bin and carries on with the dialogue.

When playing unspoken thoughts, actors don't need to worry about how to play them – if they think them deeply enough, the story will be told through their body language and on their faces.

Themes in and around the play

🖐 YOUNG PEOPLE AND GANGS

Group of friends or gang?

Everyone, whatever their age, hangs around or makes friends they have something in common with. In fact, for many young people belonging to a group of friends is very much a part of growing up.

It's these connections that also make groups or gangs. It can be about going to the same school or youth club, or coming from the same neighbourhood. Being part of a gang can give young people lots of positive things, like a sense of identity, status and even protection.

Recently, TV and newspapers have reported the rise of gangs and gang culture in the UK. Gangs of young people are often shown in a bad light and are blamed for graffiti, litter and noise. But this is not the whole picture. For many young people a gang is really about hanging out with friend and doing things together.

Discussion

What is the difference between a group of friends and a gang? What good images of gangs can you think of from films or literature? What effects have news reports on gangs had on the public?

Gangs and territory

Gangs are often based around where young people live. Arguments can start over who controls different places or territory such as local parks, youth clubs or the area around the shops. At its worst this can lead to young people fighting. It can also mean young people from one area are frightened of going to another area. It can even stop them doing things they want to, like visiting friends, going to a particular youth club or playing in the park.

Bullying, fighting and conflict over territory can have a massive impact on a young person's day-to-day life. They can be frightened of going out or of entering another gang's territory. They may not be able to use facilities, or have to walk long distances to and from school because it means crossing places they are scared of going through. This can cause stress and dent a young person's confidence.

Reports of fighting between groups of young people are also on the increase. This has happened the most in places where unemployment, low achievement at school, poverty and crime are present and there's not much for young people to do, like organised activities at youth clubs.

Discussion

What fears do the characters in Mugged have that are similar to those in the article above? Why do you think arguments over territory happen?

Teen Spirit

If only the Montagues and Capulets in *Romeo and Juliet* could have been persuaded to divert their energies into football competition or a mini-Olympics. Absurd? Particularly in doublet and hose perhaps. But today such activities are being used to break down the barriers of suspicion, harboured grievance and territorial divisions that affect young people in tough inner-city areas. Sports Relief funds are helping to support such initiatives.

Jerome Monahan

Ask pupils what 'gang' suggests. It is likely that the main images conjured up will be of a highly organised unit, with distinct hierarchies, dedicated to criminal activities and prepared to assert its authority through violence. The victims of gang warfare may also crop up. Yet recent research sponsored by the charity Leap suggests that only a minority of groups function in this highly antisocial way.

Working out where such images come from might prove interesting too. Films and television present this negative model over and over again, and newspaper reporting frequently uses the term 'gang' as shorthand for all sorts of groupings. Invite students to suggest other 'associations' that could be described as gangs.

Nor are gangs inevitably male. Recent research at one south-east London girl's school revealed patterns of allegiance and violence that shadowed the structure of local boy gangs.

Writing assignment

Another term to unravel is the word 'enemy'. Such an activity is key to the reconciliation Leap undertakes. "It is often the case that the enemies young people are defending themselves from have more in common with them than differences," explains Jessie Feinstein, the charity's gang's worker. "Many gangs are very mixed ethnically. Getting young people to recognise that their enemies are almost identical to themselves can be a crucial step in reconciliation work."

Imagine you are an 'agony aunt/uncle' for a magazine. You receive a letter from a 16-year-old who wants to join a gang. How would you persuade them that this is not the answer to their problems but may, in fact, the the cause of more?

Now read this extract from *Face* by Benjamin Zephaniah.

Mark, Martin and Matthew spotted four boys from Easmorelands and headed over to say hello. This was not Natalie's scene at all. She knew she couldn't afford to look timid, so she lifted her shoulders and held her head high as she stood around listening to the boys' small talk.

After a couple of minutes she realised that her every move was being watched by a group of three girls and she couldn't help noticing how tough they looked. All three were wearing dark blue baggy jeans. She was pretty sure they were Londoners born and bred but thought they could find a job working for the Jamaican tourist board, not simply because of their dark skin but also because of their clothing. One had a T-shirt saying 'I Love Jamaica'. Another wore a T-shirt that was a Jamaican flag and the third just had a West Ham football shirt on, but she, like the others was adorned with yellow, black and green bangles, badges and necklaces. Natalie thought they looked good but dangerous.

Natalie shifted nervously. She didn't know quite where to look but she had to put on a front. The other three girls made no attempt to hide the fact that they were on Natalie's case. They began to whisper to each other and smile as they stared at her. Natalie felt illuminated in her green satins and began to wish she had chosen clothes that weren't so loud. What are they grinning at? she wondered. Is it my clothes? My shoes? My hair? Do I look innocent? Suddenly the three girls started to walk towards Natalie. Her heart began to race; the palms of her hands began to sweat. She felt like falling apart but she held herself together.

Discussion

What sorts of clothing and hairstyle might appear to give a young person a dangerous quality? Is it better to wear neutral clothing to blend in with the crowd? What sorts of clothing do you associate with different types of young people such as Goths, townies, skaters, punks, etc?

Writing

What do you imagine is going to happen next in this extract? Carry on the narrative. Then find out what really happened in the novel.

Reconciliation

The charity Leap uses a variety of drama techniques in its reconciliation work in schools. Here are a few that have been adapted.

1. Use frozen tableaux to show what happens before, during and after a variety of situations. Reflect on alternative courses of action. You could apply this exercise to the incident in Scene One, which is described by Taylor, Dig, Leon, Soph and Mel but actually happens off-stage. In small groups, freeze-frame the moment Marky tries talking to the bullies in an attempt to get Soph's phone back. Choose at least two other moments as described in the dialogue.

2. Show the freeze frames to the rest of the class. Invite them to ask questions of the characters in-role. Hot-seat the bullies and find out why they let the situation get out of hand. Discuss how the stabbing might have been avoided.

☺☺☺ BULLYING

Bullying can be a serious problem, and it badly affects the lives of some of the characters in *Mugged*. (The bullying we see in the play happens outside school.) A useful website to visit is www.bullying.co.uk. See what advice it gives that might have been useful to the characters who are being bullied. Find out what your school's policy is over bullying and if there is a local self-defence class.

Read this extract from *Noughts and Crosses* by Malorie Blackman.

––––––

"We're only going to say this once," Lola told me icily.

"Choose who your friends are very carefully. If you don't stay away from those blankers, you'll find you don't have a single friend in this school."

"Why d'you hate them so much?" I asked, bewildered.

"I bet none of you have even spoken to a single nought before."

"Of course we have," Joanne piped up. "I've spoken to blankers lots of times – when they serve us in shops and restaurants..."

"And there are some working in our own food hall..."

"Yeah, that's right. And besides we don't need to speak to them. We see them in the news practically every other day. Everyone knows they all belong to the Liberation Militia and all they do is cause trouble and commit crimes and stuff like that..."

I stared at them, astounded. They can't really be serious, I thought, But they could obviously read what I was thinking all over my face.

"The news doesn't lie," Lola told me huffily.

"The news lies all the time. They tell us what they think we want to hear," I said. Callum had told me that. At the time I didn't fully understand what he meant. But I did now.

"Who told you that?" Joanne's eyes narrowed. "Your dad?"

"I bet it was one of your blanket friends," Lola said with scorn.

"They're blank by name and blank by nature."

"What do you mean?" I asked.

"Blank, white faces with not a hint of colour in them. Blank minds which can't hold a single original thought. Blank, blank, blank," Lola recited. "That's why they serve us and not the other way around."

"You ought to sell that horse manure worldwide. It's quality stuff. You'd make a fortune!" I sprung up.

"Noughts are people, just like us. You're the ones who are stupid and ignorant and..."

Lola gave me another slap around my face for that, but this time I was ready for it. Win or lose they weren't going to get away with it. I made a fist, drew it back and punched Lola in the stomach. She doubled over with an "Oof!" I struck out with my elbows and my fists, and my feet all at the same time, trying to make as many of my blows count before they could react. I had the element of surprise on my side, but not for long. Joanne and Lola each grabbed a flailing arm whilst Dionne straightened up to glare down on me. Dionne was the best fighter in her year and everyone knew it. But if she was expecting me to beg or cry, she'd have a long wait. She gave me a slow smile of satisfaction.

"Blanket-lover... You've had this coming for a long time." She said softly.

And then she let me have it.

Sephy, one of the two central characters, is narrating the story at the point at which the extract is taken from. She is being threatened by the girls because she refuses to give into their pressure. As you can see from the extract she has been subjected to verbal and physical bullying.

Discussion

1. How does Sephy's point of view differ from the other girls? What arguments do the girls make to try and bring Sephy round to their way of thinking?

2. Sephy believes the media is partly responsible for forming the girls' point of view. What other influences do you imagine the girls might have experienced?

Look at Scene Two of *Mugged*. Here the media is reporting the stabbing. Discuss how the reports differ from what actually happened.

Writing

Write a newspaper article about the stabbing incident that is factually correct. Look carefully at the play before you do this.

Further into the scene, a TV Reporter interviews 'gawpers'. These bystanders all appear to have a similar point of view. They focus on the negative aspects of the local school, the kids that go there, the lack of discipline and the lack of will to do anything about the situation.

Now read Scene Five. Compare the news coverage in this scene with the coverage in Scene Two. How has the media's attitude changed? Look at how the news reports have influenced the gawpers' point of view.

Discussion

How would you present the Gawpers if you were staging *Mugged*? What sort of age would they be? What would they look like? Would they be similar? Who might the TV Reporter have interviewed to encourage a more balanced point of view?

 FACTS

The information below is from *Fear and Fashion*, a government report on the use of knives and other weapons by young people published in 2004.

- 10% of boys aged 11 and 12 are reported to have carried a knife or other weapon in the previous year and 8% said they had attacked someone intending serious harm.
- By the age of 16, the figure had risen to 24% who had carried a knife and 16% who had attacked somebody intending harm.
- Pupils attending schools said that the offences typically happen at school.
- Excluded young people appear more likely to experience crime in the local area where they live and are more likely to carry weapons.

- 46% of excluded young people had admitted having carried a weapon compared to just 16% of those at school.

- The peak age for both boys and girls committing offences is 14 to 15.

- Carrying weapons is more common among those in year 10 and 11 at school.

- Boys are more likely to carry and use knives.

- The possession of a knife or other weapon can be a means of acquiring status, e.g. children who experience failure at school or other kinds of social exclusion could be looking for status by carrying a knife.

- Peer influences and fashion also seem to play a part in encouraging young people to carry knives.

- Fear and victimisation are the main reasons why young people carry and brandish knives. Young people carry knives with the intention to scare, harass or steal.

- Projects that focus on preventing or tackling the use of knives are designed to raise awareness amongst young people of the dangers of carrying knives.

Discussion

What sorts of knives are dangerous? Who is most likely to carry a knife? What are the dangers of carrying a weapon? What should you do if you know someone who has a knife?

Read the statements above. Do you agree or disagree with them? Why? What can be done about this problem?

Read this extract from Scene Four.

DIG	Soph?
SOPH	What?
DIG	About the knife.
SOPH	What about it?

Beat.

DIG   I nicked it.

SOPH   I know.

DIG   You know?

SOPH   Well, I guessed. I got here before the others that morning. I was down there, texting Leon. I saw you and Marky shoving stuff back in your bags. Then Mel and Tayl turned up.

Beat.

DIG   I got it from the art shop. I was after felt-tips but the bloke in there, he's such a suspicious bastard, always looking at you like you're going to do something, but he had to answer the phone so I just grabbed the box and ran. I wasn't after a knife at all, I was after felt-tips.

Beat.

I made Marky swap it for fags so I could give them to you.

Beat.

Why didn't you tell the others?

SOPH   You didn't tell the police about my mum's phone.

Beat.

DIG   How do you tell the truth? About what actually happened? You know, tell the actual truth. It's all so complicated.

Soph was more afraid of telling the truth to her mum about the phone than lying to the police. But the two resolve to tell the truth.

The other big untruth in *Mugged* is the way Marky is portrayed at the end of the play by the media and the people who hardly knew him. Discuss why his finer qualities were exaggerated once he was dead.

If someone is constantly made to feel inferior, bad even, that person is far more likely to consider getting even. Read this second extract from *Noughts and Crosses*. This time the other central character in the novel, Callum, narrates it.

"Let me see your ticket."

I handed it over.

"Where did you get the money to buy this kind of ticket?"

I looked up at them, but didn't speak. What was there to say? They had the scent of blood in their nostrils and I didn't stand a chance, no matter what I said or did. So why bother?

"I asked you a question," Moustaches reminded me.

As if I'd forgotten.

"Did you buy this ticket?" Moustache's accomplice asked.

The truth or prevarication? What was Sephy thinking? I couldn't see her. The no-brains brothers were in the way. If only I could see her face.

"I asked you a question, boy. Did you buy this ticket?"

"No, I didn't," I replied.

"Come with us please."

Time to get my posterior pummelled. Time to get my derriere dealt with. Time to get my bum bounced off the train.

How dare a nought sit in first class? It's outrageous. It's a scandal. It's disgusting. Disinfect that seat at once.

"Officer, he's with me. I bought the tickets." Sephy was on her feet. "Is there a problem?"

"And you are?"

"Persephone Hadley. My dad's the Home Office Minister Kamal Hadley. Callum is my friend," Sephy said firmly.

"He is?"

"Yes, he is." Sephy's voice had a steely tone to it that I'd never heard before. Not from her anyway.

"I see," said Moustaches.

"I can give you my father's private number. I'm sure he'll sort all this in a moment. Or you'll be able to talk to Juno Ayelette his personal secretary."

Careful, Sephy. I'm tripping over all those names you're dropping.

"So is there a problem, officer?" repeated Sephy.

Sniff! Sniff! Was I imagining things or was there the definite hint of a threat in the air? And I wasn't the only one to smell it. Moustaches handed back my pass.

"Would you like to see my ID as well?" Sephy held out her pass.

"That won't be necessary, Miss Hadley." Moustaches almost bowed.

"I really don't mind." Sephy thrust it under Moustaches nose.

"That won't be necessary," Moustaches repeated looking straight at Sephy. He didn't even glance at her ID card.

Sephy sat back down again. "Well, if you're sure."

She turned to look out of the window. Moustaches was effectively dismissed. Sephy's mother would've been proud. Moustaches glared at me like it was my fault. He'd been humiliated, and by a child no less, and he wanted to take it out on someone. Sephy was off-limits, and now, so was I. He was burning to re-establish his authority but he couldn't. Not with us anyway. Moustaches and his colleague moved off down the carriage. Sephy turned to me and winked.

"You OK?" she asked.

"Fine," I lied. "Wasn't that fun?"

Notice how in the previous extract we heard Callum's unspoken feelings. Read the following extract from Scene One of *Mugged*.

LEON And what if he recognised Marky? Did he recognise you, Marky?

MARKY Dunno.

They start talking over each other:

MEL He knows where Marky lives...

SOPH *(crying)* My mum's going to throw me out...

TAYLOR Over a poxy phone? You're joking me...

MEL She will, too...

SOPH You don't know what she's like...

LEON She's a nutter, man...

TAYLOR Get over it girl, you ain't going to get it back now...

MEL *(shoves **Taylor**)* You get over it...

TAYLOR Hey...

SOPH *(to **Leon**, crying, hitting him)* She is not a nutter...

MARKY I'll talk to him, Soph, all right?

This shuts them up.

Look at the punctuation in the extract. When they start talking over each other you'll notice they don't finish their sentences. This means the dialogue moves at a fast pace and with urgency. The actors playing these characters will have to pick up their cues quickly. But it's important for the actors to finish the thought they're having in their head.

Writing

Complete the sentences in the extract from *Mugged* above. Write down the unfinished thoughts.

ACTIVITIES MAPPING

English Framework Objectives (Year 7/8/9)

Page Number	Word (W) & Sentence (S) Level	Text Level		Speaking & Listening
		Reading	Writing	
65				(7) 13
69		(7) 1 (8) 3	(7) 2	
71	(7) S15 (8) S12		(7) 1 (9) 1	
73				(7) 15, 16, 18 (8) 14, 15, 16 (9) 11, 12, 14
74				(7) 15, 16, 17, 18 (8) 14, 15, 16 (9) 11, 12, 14
76			(7) 2	
77				(7) 15, 18 (8) 14 (9) 14
78				(7) 11, 12, 14 (8) 10, 12 (9) 9

Learning Objectives (Year 7/8/9)

79						**(7)** 11, 12, 14 **(8)** 10, 12
80						**(7)** 11, 12, 14 **(8)** 10, 12
81				(7) 1		**(7)** 11, 12, 14, 15, 16, 17, 18 **(8)** 10, 12, 14, 15, 16 **(9)** 11, 12, 14
83		**(7)** S17 **(8)** S9 **(9)** 9		**(7)** 1, 10, 14 **(8)** 12 **(9)** 9, 11		**(7)** 11, 12, 14 **(8)** 10, 12
84						**(7)** 11, 12, 14 **(8)** 10, 12
85						**(7)** 11, 12, 14 **(8)** 10, 12
86				(7) 1		**(7)** 11, 12, 14, 16 **(8)** 10, 12 **(9)** 14
88						**(7)** 11, 12, 14 **(8)** 10, 12
89				(7) 6		

National Theatre Workshops are available to support your work on this play.

There are two options available for you:

Visit the National Theatre on London's Southbank to attend a teachers' one-day INSET on the play facilitated by a director and the writer of the play. These INSET days are programmed regularly throughout the academic year and a limited number of places are available.

Host a one-day workshop at your school led by a National Theatre director and the author of the play. The day will be spent working with your staff and students on the text of this play.

For further information on prices, booking a workshop, and forthcoming dates of INSETs please contact Connections Enterprises on 0207 452 3728.

You can also:

Participate in the current Connections Programme and have access to the newest set of plays. See the Connections website for details.

For information on all the workshops and other projects about new writing for young people offered by Connections Enterprises for your school visit:

www.nationaltheatre.org.uk/connections/enterprises

The Exam

Andy Hamilton

The Exam is a comic look at the pressures put on young people by parents and teachers.

Andrew, Chas and Bea are three candidates of mixed ability who find themselves holed up in the same exam hall waiting for their papers to arrive.

As the wait lengthens, each has to survive a powerful barrage of self-doubt, parental pressure and adult incompetence. They must come to terms with themselves, their peers and parents – provoked and helped by 'Ex', the mysterious, disembodied voice of the exam.

The Willow Pattern

Judith Johnson

The Willow Pattern tells the story behind the willow-pattern plates that found their way to Europe in the 19th century.

Knoon-She is the much cherished daughter of a powerful Mandarin. He wants her to marry TA-Jin, a brainless warrior. But Knoon She has fallen in love with her father's secretary, Chang, and is determined to be with him despite knowing that her father would disapprove. When one day the Mandarin happens upon them kissing in the gardens, Chang is forced to flee the palace.

Encompassing poetry, story-telling, proverbs and a little martial arts, The Willow Pattern is accessible, funny, moving and thought-provoking. A great drama text for Year 7 up.